AMERICAN TALL TALES

Paul Bunyan

Retold by M. J. York ❧ Illustrated by Michael Garland

The Child's World®
1980 Lookout Drive • Mankato, MN 56003-1705
800-599-READ • www.childsworld.com

Acknowledgments
The Child's World®: Mary Berendes, Publishing Director
The Design Lab: Kathleen Petelinsek, Design
Red Line Editorial: Editorial direction

ISBN 9781614732112
LCCN 2012932868

Printed in the United States of America
Mankato, MN
July 2012
PA02124

Way back in the olden days, when the big woods stretched clear across America from coast to coast, a bouncing baby boy was born in Maine. This baby was called Paul Bunyan, and he was a mighty big boy.

Baby Paul was so big, it took five storks to bring him when he was born. By the time he was a week old, he was wearin' his father's clothes. When he was hungry, he drank all the milk out of twelve cows. When he got the hiccups, everyone ran out of their houses thinkin' it was an earthquake. When he sneezed, folks had to open their umbrellas all the way in California.

When Paul Bunyan grew up, he knew there was only one job for him. Folks were a'movin' West in those days, and they all needed houses. They needed firewood and furniture and all kinds of things made of wood. And Paul Bunyan knew he would be the biggest and best logger in the country.

Paul Bunyan set up his logging camp on the Onion River. He had so many men in his camp, they worked in three groups. One group was always goin' to work, one was workin', and one was a'comin' back. Paul's voice was so loud, all the men had to wear earmuffs so they wouldn't go deaf.

It took a lot of food to feed all those men. The cook set up a pancake griddle bigger than a skating rink. And that's how his assistants greased it up—skatin' round the griddle with bacon strapped to their feet. The cook was nearsighted, though. One day, he put blasting powder in the batter instead of baking powder. Those pancakes blew the roof clear off the cookhouse!

Paul Bunyan had a mighty big axe. It was so big, he could chop down forty acres of trees in one swing. One day, he got tired while he was headin' back to camp, so he let his axe drag behind him. That axe opened up a big ol' crack folks now call the Grand Canyon.

Now, the winter of '47 was colder than the coldest winter the old graybeards could remember. It was so cold, the words froze in the air as you said them. Then there was a huge chatter in the spring when they all thawed at the same time. It was so cold, even the snow turned blue.

But the snow and the cold didn't bother Paul Bunyan. Why not? Because when Paul Bunyan walked, the snowbanks were so afraid of getting stepped on, they moved clear out of his way.

So Paul Bunyan was walkin' out in the woods during the winter of the blue snow. The snowbanks moved away, and under the biggest snowbank was a big, blue baby ox. The ox was born white, but he turned blue on account of the blue snow.

Paul cradled the ox in his arms and took him home. The ox gave Paul Bunyan's face a big, sticky lick, and they became great friends.

Paul called the blue ox Babe, and the name stuck even when Babe grew bigger than Paul. Babe was so big, it took forty-seven axe handles to measure between his horns. He was so long, if you or I stood at his tail, we'd need a telescope to see his nose. When Babe wanted a snack, he ate thirty bales of hay in one bite, wire and all.

With Babe around, Paul Bunyan could work twice as fast. As quick as Paul cut down a tree, Babe hauled it away. When Paul Bunyan wanted to skin a log, he hitched Babe up to one end and held the bark himself at the other end. Babe would pull the log out, clean as a whistle, leaving Paul holding the bark.

Around the camp, the men hung up their shirts to dry on Babe's horns. But Babe's most important job was making the logging roads straight by pulling out their twists and turns.

One time, Paul Bunyan and Babe went out to the Dakotas to do some logging. They worked so fast and so hard, they cut down all the trees there. But, since they were headed home again, they decided to clean up before they left. Paul Bunyan pounded all the tree stumps down into the ground, and that's why to this day there are so few trees in the Dakotas.

After a while, Babe got sick
of haulin' logs all the way down
to the Gulf of Mexico. So Paul
Bunyan decided there should be
a canal runnin' all the way from
Minnesota to Louisiana. He dug
the mighty canal. When the
dirt went over his left shoulder,
it made the Rocky Mountains.
And when the dirt went over
his right shoulder, it made the
Appalachian Mountains. Babe
kicked over his water bucket to
fill the canal. And today logs can

float from north to south on the Mississippi River.

   After many years of logging together, Paul and Babe's work was done. So they packed up and moved north to Alaska. Listen carefully, and you can probably still hear Paul yelling "TIMBER!"

BEYOND THE STORY

Paul Bunyan is a type of story known as a tall tale. Tall tales are set in real-life places, like the American West, but contain fictional and exaggerated elements. To exaggerate something is to make it larger, more exciting, scarier, or otherwise than it would be in real life.

Some tall tales are based on true events or actual people. Others are completely made-up, or fiction. In the case of the *Paul Bunyan* story, the main character and his ox are fictional. No history of a real-life Paul Bunyan exists. You could call Paul Bunyan larger than life!

There are so many exaggerated elements in this tall tale that it's hard to count them all. A few are: that Paul Bunyan was so large that he blew birds across the country when he sneezed, that he created the Grand Canyon with his dragging ax, and that he found and raised a baby blue ox that grew up to be as large as he was. What other exaggerations can you find?

Despite all the fiction, the character of Paul Bunyan exists in a land that's very real. He has a job as a logger, or lumberjack. Lumberjacks are often very large men as they have to swing big axes and haul heavy lumber. He travels from Maine to Minnesota to Oregon and back—all real places in the United States. And he chops trees to float down rivers to be made into lumber (wood to build houses and furniture) at sawmills—just like a real lumberjack would.

ABOUT THE AUTHOR

M. J. York has an undergraduate degree in English and history and a master's degree in library science. M. J. lives in Minnesota and works as a children's book editor. She has always been fascinated by myths, legends, and fairy tales from around the world.

ABOUT THE ILLUSTRATOR

Michael Garland is a best-selling author and illustrator with thirty books to his credit. He has received numerous awards and his recent book, *Miss Smith and the Haunted Library*, made the New York Times Best Sellers list. Michael has illustrated for celebrity authors such as James Patterson and Gloria Estefan, and his book *Christmas Magic* has become a season classic. Michael lives in New York with his family.